Angelica shook her head in disbelief. "You babies are so dumb! Of course there will be people in Tommy's house. Except it won't be Tommy's house anymore. It will belong to New People. They'll paint the walls different colors, and bring in their own furniture. The New People might have babies, too. *New* Babies!" Angelica smiled. She liked the idea of having a whole new group of babies to boss around.

Tommy gasped. "No New People are taking over *my* house!" he declared.

Rugrats Chapter Books

Tommy's Last Stand

Based on the TV series *Rugrats*® created by Arlene Klasky, Gabor Csupo, and Paul Germain as seen on Nickelodeon®

ISBN 0-439-11546-9

12 11 10 9 8 7 6 5 4 3 2 1   9/9 0 1 2 3 4/0

Printed in the U.S.A.   40

First Scholastic printing, October 1999

Tommy's Last Stand

by Nancy Krulik
illustrated by the Thompson Bros.

SCHOLASTIC INC.
New York   Toronto   London   Auckland   Sydney
Mexico City   New Delhi   Hong Kong

Chapter 1

"CHARGE!"

Tommy Pickles watched as the soldiers on horseback raced out of the fort and swooped down onto the open prairie. The general at the head of the thundering troop raised the flag and waved his arm. The horses galloped even faster.

Tommy loved watching old black-and-white movies on TV with his grandfather. They were so exciting. There was always someone shouting, cheering, or riding horses.

Tommy's grandfather grinned at his grandson. "Now this is what I call a movie, scout!" he said. "When I was young, I had to trudge *fifteen* miles just to get to the movie theater! But it was worth it. Those movies were filled with real heroes. Not like the lovey-dovey actors you see in movies these days."

Grandpa pointed to the screen. "You see the men with the big hats riding on horseback? They're protecting the fort from the bad guys who want to take it over," he explained. "Don't worry. Those guys are in the U.S. Army. They're the good guys—and the good guys *always* win!"

Just then Tommy's mother, Didi, walked into the room. She looked at the

TV screen and shook her head. "Pop, I don't think this is the kind of movie Tommy should watch. According to Dr. Lipschitz's baby advice books, young children can be frightened by loud noises on TV."

Grandpa Lou didn't change the channel. Instead, he changed the subject. "Didi, can I have a bottle of soda, *pleeease?*" he asked.

Didi sighed. She went into the kitchen and came back with a bottle of cola.

"Hey, this is warm," Tommy's grandfather blurted as he took a sip.

"Sorry, but there's no room for your soda bottles in the refrigerator," Didi said as she headed toward the laundry room to fold yet another load of laundry. "Dil's baby bottles are taking up space in there now."

Dil was Tommy's baby brother. Ever

since he was born, there hadn't been room for much of anything anymore. No matter where Tommy went in his house, he bumped into Dil's stuff. Piles of Dil's diapers filled the laundry room. His baby swing took up a whole corner of the living room. And his pacifiers always fell under the couch cushions!

But the biggest problem was the double stroller Didi bought. The man at the baby store had promised her that the stroller wouldn't take up much space because it folded up with the click of a button. But Tommy's parents never could seem to find the button. So they just left it set up in the TV room.

Suddenly the basement door flew open. Tommy gasped. A monster was coming up the stairs! He had a big plastic mask over his head. His hands and arms were covered with thick black rubber.

The monster walked closer and closer. He raised his rubber-coated claws, lifted off his plastic mask, and reached for Tommy!

Tommy took one look at the monster's face . . . and smiled. That wasn't a monster after all! It was just his dad. He was dressed funny because he was working on his latest invention.

"This invention will put Pickles Industries on the map!" Stu told his son. "It's called the Octopus. See, it's got eight arms, which means it can do eight different things at once, like throw a ball with one arm while turning a jump rope with the other, play patty-cake while picking up socks . . . hey, it can even shoot water out of its arm to cool you off on summer days!"

Stu tried to demonstrate how the Octopus worked. He threw a ball at one

of the machine's arms. He turned a jump rope with another. Stu was so busy with his invention that he didn't notice his wife walk into the room with a huge pile of laundry. As Stu tried to show how the Octopus's sprinkler system might work, he accidentally kicked the double stroller. It rolled across the room—right into Didi!

"Owww!" she cried as the laundry flew out of her hands.

A white crib sheet landed on Tommy's head. Tommy struggled to get it off his head.

"Arf! Arf! Arf!" Tommy's dog, Spike, came bounding into the room. He took one look at the moving white sheet and growled. Then he raced out of the room as fast as he could. As Spike ran off, his tail knocked over a tall tower of blocks that Tommy had built. The multicolored blocks skittered across the floor.

"Ouch!" Tommy's dad yelled as he tripped on one of the blocks and fell onto the coffee table. The table turned over and crashed into the bookshelf! *Boom!* Piles of Dr. Lipschitz's baby advice books and videotapes fell to the floor.

"That settles it!" Didi declared as she gathered up the books. "This house is just too small for all of us. It's time to move to a bigger house!"

Chapter 2

The next morning, right after breakfast, Tommy's family piled into the car and went for a drive. They stopped in front of a small office building. A lady with flaming red hair and lips stuck her face through the car window.

"Okay, Mr. and Mrs. Pickles, just follow my car," she told them. "We have lots of homes that fit your size and price requirements. Although, of course, you can get a bigger house if you add just a few more dollars to your budget."

"Not another dime, Mrs. Fussbinder!" Stu declared.

Mrs. Fussbinder got into her long red car and drove off. Stu followed close behind until they reached a tall white house with blue trim on the shutters.

"What a lovely house!" Didi exclaimed as she got out of the car.

"Now, you're sure this is within our price range?" Stu asked Mrs. Fussbinder as they followed her up the walk.

"Did you notice the yard?" she asked, avoiding Stu's question. "It's certainly large enough for two active young boys."

Tommy looked up at the house. It sure seemed big. The trees looked really big too. In fact everything about this place was big. Too big!

Then Tommy spotted a house that was just his size. It was built right into the lower branches of a tree! While the grown-ups talked, Tommy toddled over toward the wooden tree house.

I wonder what's in there? he asked himself. There was only one way to find out. Tommy began to climb the wobbly rope ladder that hung from the tree house. But when he reached the top and tried to climb inside, his foot got caught on the last rung.

"Ugh!" Tommy groaned as he kicked and tugged on the ladder. Finally his foot came free. But all that kicking and tugging loosened the ladder from the nails that attached it to the tree house, and it dropped to the ground as Tommy climbed in.

Inside, the tree house was completely empty except for an old picnic blanket and a few paper cups. Tommy crawled toward a window.

"Wow!" he exclaimed. "This is really

high. Maybe I can see my house from here." He poked his head out of the window and looked straight out. But nothing seemed familiar. Suddenly Tommy felt alone and far from home. It was not a good feeling.

Then Tommy heard a door close down below. His mom was carrying Dil to the car. It was time to go. Tommy crawled toward the entrance and got ready to climb down. But the ladder wasn't there anymore! How was he going to get down?

Just then Tommy spotted his dad, who also caught sight of him. "There you are," said Stu. "Don't worry, I'm coming to get you."

Stu tried to climb the tree. But the branches were too high for him to grab on to. "Didi, can you come over?" he called.

Didi handed Dil to Mrs. Fussbinder and came running over. "Oh, my," Didi said, when she saw Tommy in the tree house. "How are we going to get him down?"

"Climb up on my shoulders," Stu said. Didi did as she was told and lifted Tommy from the tree house.

"I don't blame you for wanting to get away from Mrs. Fussbinder," Stu told his son, "but next time can you take me with you?"

"Oh, Stu," said Didi.

"Now, this house is slightly smaller than the last one, but it is in your price range," Mrs. Fussbinder told Stu and Didi as they got out of the car in front of a different house.

This house didn't look any smaller to Tommy. But the yard sure did. There was no grass at all. Just a slab of concrete.

"Come on inside," Mrs. Fussbinder said as she opened the front door. "The kitchen window has a lovely view of the neighbor's yard."

"I'd like to see the size of the family room," Didi said.

Tommy watched his family follow Mrs. Fussbinder into the next room. But he didn't want to see the rest of this house. He just wanted to go home—his *own* home.

Tommy walked over to the back door, which had a dog door at the bottom. It swung open, and he crawled through. He sat down in the yard. "I don't wanna live in a new house," Tommy said sadly. "If we live here, my friends won't know where I am. I might never see them again."

Slam! Tommy heard the sound of the back door closing. His parents and Mrs. Fussbinder were leaving.

"Ready to go, sweetie?" Didi asked as she picked Tommy up. "There's only one more house to see. I'm sorry. I'll bet this house hunting is pretty boring for you."

Tommy simply hugged his mother a little bit tighter.

They arrived at a house that was at the end of a long street. It was brown with green shutters. A white picket fence surrounded the yard.

"This looks beautiful!" Didi exclaimed as Mrs. Fussbinder rang the doorbell. A woman answered the door. In her arms she carried a little girl about Tommy's age.

"Hello, we've been expecting you," the woman said. She smiled at Tommy. "You look hungry," she said. Then she turned to Didi. "Would your older son like to share some crackers with Tabitha?"

"I'm sure Tommy would love to," Didi agreed. They followed the woman into a big playroom. The mothers put their children into the playpen.

"You two get to know each other while I get the crackers," Tabitha's mother said as she left the room.

"I love this house," Tommy heard his mother say as she followed close behind.

Once the grown-ups were gone, Tabitha began to cry.

"Don't worry, they'll be back," Tommy assured her.

"I'm not crying because my mom left the room. I'm crying because your mom likes my house," Tabitha explained.

"What's wrong with that?" Tommy asked her.

"That means your parents might live

in my house. Then it wouldn't be my house anymore. It would be your house," Tabitha told Tommy.

"Where would your house be?" Tommy asked her.

"I don't know!" Tabitha sobbed.

"Don't worry. I'll make sure my parents don't live in your house," Tommy declared.

"How are you going to do that?" Tabitha asked.

"I'll make sure we stay in our own houses," Tommy replied confidently.

"But how?"

Tommy didn't answer. He wasn't sure how he was going to make his family stay put. He just knew he had to.

Chapter 3

The next morning, while Tommy was playing with his blocks, the doorbell rang. Didi answered the door. Tommy's best friend, Chuckie, and Chuckie's dad, Chas, were standing on the porch.

"Oh, Chas, it's you," Tommy's mother said. "I thought you were the real estate agent."

"Is she bringing people here today?" he asked. "I only need to drop Chuckie off for a few hours. . . ."

"That's okay," Didi assured him. "The kids can play in the yard while Stu and I get the house ready. Pop can watch them."

While Grandpa Lou napped in the yard, Chuckie asked Tommy, "What's a real stake agent? I've never even seen a fake stake agent."

"A real stake agent is a lady who walks into people's houses," Tommy told Chuckie.

"Why does she do that?" Chuckie asked.

"To see if the growed-ups like them," Tommy replied. "If the growed-ups like the house they walk into, they'll live there."

"Why is she coming here?"

Tommy sighed. "Because my mom and dad want us to live in a new house."

"A NEW HOUSE!" Chuckie exclaimed.

"But, Tommy, you *can't* go to a new house! If you go, maybe we won't be bestest friends anymore. Maybe we won't . . ." Chuckie began to cry. He sobbed so loud, he didn't even hear the doorbell ring.

"Oh, Chuckie, don't cry," Tommy's mother said as she came running over. "Your dad will be back soon. And look, Phil and Lil are here!"

Chuckie wiped the tears away from his glasses and tried to stop crying.

"What's the matter?" Phil and Lil asked.

"He doesn't want me to go to a new house," Tommy answered.

"Are you—" Phil began.

"Going away?" Lil finished her twin brother's question.

"Not if I can help it," Tommy replied.

"But I always know my house is next to yours," said Phil.

"If you're not here, how are we going to know where *our* house is?" Lil wondered out loud.

"How are you going to stop your mom and dad from making you go, Tommy?" Chuckie asked as he caught his breath.

Before Tommy could answer, his three-year-old cousin, Angelica, appeared. "Hey, I heard you're not going to be here much longer," she said.

Chuckie started crying again.

"Tommy, if you're not here, what's gonna happen to this house?" Phil asked.

"Won't it be lonely without anybody inside it?" Lil wondered.

Angelica shook her head in disbelief. "You babies are so dumb! Of course there will be people in Tommy's house. Except it won't be Tommy's house anymore. It will belong to New People.

They'll paint the walls different colors, and bring in their own furniture. The New People might have babies, too. *New Babies!*" Angelica smiled. She liked the idea of having a whole new group of babies to boss around.

Tommy gasped. "No New People are taking over *my* house!" he declared.

"How's a baby like you gonna stop them?" Angelica taunted.

Tommy thought for a minute. Then he smiled. He had a plan. "I'm joining the army," Tommy replied bravely. "I'm gonna 'tect my fort, I mean, my house."

"What do you do in the army, Tommy?" Chuckie asked him.

"You ride horses and yell a lot," Tommy explained.

"How does that 'tect your house?" Chuckie asked.

"I dunno," Tommy answered. "But

Grandpa said that the army always wins."

Tommy really hoped his Grandpa was right.

Chapter 4

"We'll be in your army too!" Phil and Lil declared together.

"Thanks, you guys," Tommy said. "How about you, Chuckie?"

Chuckie hesitated. "I don't know about this, Tommy," he said finally. "The growed-ups can get pretty mad at us for yelling and everything."

"But if we don't, the New People will take over Tommy's house," Lil told him.

Chuckie had no choice. "I'm in the army now," he said.

"Good," Tommy declared. "Now the first thing we need is some horses." Tommy walked over to a tree and picked up his prized stallion. The horse was really just a long wooden stick with a plastic horse head attached, but it was all he had.

"CHARGE!" Tommy shouted. He began riding his horse around the yard.

Tommy's friends galloped behind him. They shouted as loudly as they could. Angelica laughed as she watched the babies pretend to ride on horses. "Whatcha babies doin'?" she asked.

" 'Tecting the fort!" Tommy told her.

"Dumb babies," muttered Angelica.

After a while Tommy, Chuckie, Phil, and Lil grew tired. They sat down to rest.

"Why do your mommy and daddy

want a new house, anyway?" Chuckie asked Tommy.

"They say we need a bigger house," Tommy replied.

"How big?" Phil and Lil asked.

Tommy stretched his arms as high as he could. "Really, really big," Tommy said.

Angelica's eyes grew wide. "You mean you're gonna move into a big house?" she asked in astonishment. "Maybe even bigger than my house?"

Tommy nodded.

Angelica jumped to her feet. "That can't happen!" she declared. "Your house can't be bigger than mine! I'm bigger than you!"

She thought for a minute. "Tell ya what, babies," Angelica finally said. "I'm gonna help you save Tommy's house. You're all members of Angelica's Army. I'm the general, and you're the soldiers.

From now on you do as I say."

"This isn't any different from *not* being in the army," Chuckie whispered to Tommy.

"No talking in the ranks!" Angelica cried out. "The first thing we need are uniforms. You babies wait here. I'll be right back!"

Angelica went into the house. A few minutes later she came out carrying four metal pots. "These are your helmets," she explained. "Put them on. It's time to begin your basic paining."

"What's that?" Tommy asked as he placed the pot on his head.

"That's when you practice for dangerous army missions. You have to be ready for anything—the desert, the jungle . . ."

"But we're just staying in the yard," Tommy told his cousin.

"Don't argue with the general!"

Angelica barked. "Just for that you have to do twenty push-ups."

"What are push-ups?" Tommy asked.

"I don't know," answered Angelica. "But when I find out, you are going to do twenty of them! Now march over to that sandbox, all of you! Hut, two, three, four."

The soldiers did as they were told. When they reached the sandbox, they stood and waited for their next order.

"This is the desert," Angelica said, pointing to the sandbox. "When you are in the desert, you have to stay low to hide from your enemies. Now, cross the desert on your bellies."

"What are you going to do, Angelica?" Lil asked.

"Watch you babies," Angelica replied. "Generals don't have to do basic paining. They might mess up their pigtails!"

"How do you know so much about the army?" Tommy asked.

"Grandpa Lou is my grandpa too, you know," Angelica replied. "You're not the only one who has to sit through those boring old movies."

Tommy stepped into the box, got down, on his belly, and slithered like a snake across the sandbox. Phil and Lil followed him. Chuckie stood at the edge. He didn't like the idea of lying in the sand.

"MOVE IT!" Angelica shouted. Chuckie tried to climb into the sandbox. But he tripped and landed facedown.

"Chuckie, are you all right?" Tommy asked.

"Hvv stth mtthh," Chuckie replied.

"What did he say?" Phil wondered.

Chuckie sat up. His face was covered with sand. He stuck out his tongue. It was covered with sand too. He used his sleeve to wipe the sand from his mouth.

"I said I have sand in my mouth," Chuckie told them.

"Okay, babies, that's enough desert paining," Angelica ordered. "Now it's time to move into the jungle. In the jungle you have to be prepared for wild animals."

Angelica looked around the yard. She spotted Spike sleeping under a tree. "There's one now. You have to walk quietly through the jungle and pass that fierce sleeping animal without waking him up. Ready? Go!"

The soldiers did as they were told. They tiptoed through the grass and over to Spike. Then they darted past him to the other side of the tree.

"Arf! Arf! Arf!" Spike suddenly woke up. The dog took one look at Chuckie's sand-covered face and ran inside the house.

"Not bad, not bad," Angelica said as she walked over to the babies. She pretended to look at a watch. "Hmm . . . it's chow time," she announced. "You guys have to learn to work together. So here's your mission: Go into the kitchen and get some food."

The soldiers were eager. They had worked hard, and now they were hungry. As they entered the living room, they spotted Grandpa Lou in his chair.

"How are we going to get past him?" Lil asked Tommy.

"Shhh," Tommy whispered. He crawled up to his grandfather.

Zzzz. Zzzz.

"It's okay, he's asleep," Tommy told the others as he crawled toward the kitchen. Chuckie, Lil, and Phil followed close behind.

In the kitchen Tommy found a box of chocolate chip cookies on the table. A few slipped out as he grabbed the box.

Chuckie picked them up and stuffed them into his pockets. The babies then quickly ran out.

"We did it, Angelica!" Phil and Lil exclaimed. Tommy handed her the cookies.

"Good work, babies," Angelica replied. She fished out a cookie from the box. "Hey, these are pretty good. I'll have another."

"What about us, Angelica?" Phil asked.

"No way! This is general's food," Angelica replied with her mouth full.

Tommy put his hands on his hips. "That's not fair—"

His sentence was cut short by the sound of a car pulling into the driveway. "It's the real stake lady!" Tommy told the others.

Angelica and the babies watched as

Mrs. Fussbinder got out of the car. A man and a woman also got out of the car.

This could only mean one thing: There was no more time for basic paining. The enemy had arrived!

Chapter 5

"What do we do now?" Chuckie asked nervously.

"We 'tect the house," Tommy told him. "And, Chuckie, you're just the baby to do it—you're holding our 'munition!"

Chuckie looked at his hands. He wasn't holding anything. "Where am I holding the 'munition?" he finally asked.

"In your pockets," Tommy told him. "Come on."

Chuckie followed Tommy to the front porch.

"Take out the cookies and put them by the door, Chuckie," Tommy said.

Chuckie reached into his pockets and took out what were once perfectly fine cookies. Now they were just a mess of crumbs and melted chocolate chips.

"Ugh," said Chuckie as he spread the cookie remains on the porch.

"That's perfect, Chuckie," Tommy said. Surely this would make Mrs. Fussbinder turn away.

But Tommy was wrong. The grown-ups stepped right over Chuckie's mess and walked into the house. They didn't even bat an eye at the ants that were gathering to feast on the cookies.

Angelica's Army wasn't giving up that easily. Quickly they followed the New People into the house. Tommy, Phil, and

Lil raced to the laundry room. Chuckie sat on the couch while Angelica went to spy on the grown-ups.

"Let's start upstairs," Didi told the couple.

"Why are you going upstairs?" Angelica asked Didi.

"To show them the bedrooms," her aunt replied.

"Angelica, why don't you go play with the other kids?" Stu suggested. But Angelica wouldn't leave. She had to make sure Tommy didn't move into a house that was bigger than hers.

While his mother was upstairs with Mrs. Fussbinder, Tommy and the twins prepared for a sneak attack on the enemy. They gathered weapons in the laundry room and waited in the hallway. Before long they heard the *thump, thump, thump* of people coming down the stairs.

"Aaaaaahhhhh!" Tommy shouted as he leaped from his hiding place. He and the twins began throwing balled-up socks, shirts, and underpants toward Mrs. Fussbinder and the New People.

But the attack didn't scare anyone. "Have you been in the laundry again?" Didi asked Tommy sweetly.

Just then a cry came from Dil's room.

"I'll only be a minute," Didi said as she ran off. She returned with Dil in her arms.

"He just woke up," she explained as she handed Dil his bottle.

Tommy watched Dil shake his bottle in the air. *Whoosh!* A stream of baby formula shot out of the bottle. The formula flew into the air and landed with a plop right on the woman's silk blouse. It left a big stain.

Yay, Dil! Tommy thought. What a

great secret weapon you turned out to be! Tommy was sure the woman would be so mad, she'd stomp right out of the house.

But the woman didn't get angry. She grinned at Dil and blotted the stain with a tissue. "This house is adorable," she said to Didi. "We want to live here!"

Oh, no! What was the army going to do now?

Chapter 6

"Do you have any other plans?" Phil asked Tommy.

"We need another secret weapon!" Tommy declared.

"Where are we gonna get that?" Lil asked.

"Come with me!" Tommy said as he headed toward the basement.

Phil and Lil followed Tommy down the basement stairs. A little later they

were back up, dragging Stu's Octopus behind them. As soon as they reached the top of the stairs, Tommy gave the order.

"Turn on the 'topus now!" he shouted.

Lil turned on the machine. It started to move. One of its tentacles began turning around and around, faster and faster, until *wham!* The whirling arm knocked over the lamp. The lamp shade fell right on Spike's head.

"Yip, yip, yip," Spike cried as he ran around the room trying to get the lamp shade off his head. He barreled into the woman, who fell backward and landed on her bottom.

The Octopus rolled toward the wall. *Bam!* Two tentacles that were playing patty-cake bashed two fist-sized holes through the wall.

The grown-ups watched in horror.

"Do something, Mr. Pickles!" Mrs. Fussbinder shouted as she ducked out of the way of a swinging Octopus tentacle.

Tommy giggled. He watched the longest arm of all stretch out as long as it could.

"Look out!" Stu shouted. "The machine's going to blow!"

Whoosh! The Octopus began spraying green and orange baby food around the room. Strained peas and carrots flew in every direction.

"It's the sprinkler function," Stu explained. "Someone filled the interior hose with baby food!" He crawled along the floor, keeping his head low to avoid being hit by one of the Octopus's tentacles. Finally he was able to switch the machine off.

"Heh, heh," Stu laughed nervously. "I guess it still has a few bugs."

Mrs. Fussbinder looked at the broken wall, the frenzied dog, and the stained carpets. "I-I-I'm sure Mr. and Mrs. P-Pick-Pickles will re-re-repair any d-d-damage—" she stammered.

The New People didn't let her finish. "No, thank you," the woman said quickly. She ran for the door.

"I think we'll look elsewhere," the man agreed as he raced off.

Tommy smiled and happily waved good-bye as Mrs. Fussbinder ran to catch up with them.

As soon as Mrs. Fussbinder and her clients had left, Tommy's parents began to clean the house.

"I'll get the spot remover," Didi said, heading for the hall closet. Suddenly she

cried out, "Oh, Stu, come look!"

Stu rushed over, expecting to see another big mess.

"Look at that," said Didi, pointing to some markings on the wall.

Stu bent to take a closer look. "Tommy's growth chart," he muttered softly.

Didi nodded. "We haven't filled that in since Dil was born. We should start doing that again . . . and we'll need to make one for Dil, too."

"You know, Didi, I've been thinking—" Stu began to say.

"Me too," Didi said. "We can't move. There are too many memories here. . . ."

"We'll make it work somehow," Stu agreed.

In the living room the babies cheered.

"Did you hear that, guys?" Tommy exclaimed. "We're staying in this house!

We won the war! My grandpa was right—the good guys always win!"

Angelica was pleased. Her house was still the biggest one. Then she remembered.

"Hey, wait a second," she said. Angelica stood tall in front of the babies. "It was because of me that we won. And it isn't over yet, babies. I'm still in charge here and I—"

But the babies were too busy cheering to pay any attention to Angelica.

About the Author

Nancy Krulik is the author of more than fifty books for children and young adults, including a few based on the hit Nickelodeon television series, *Rugrats* and *CatDog*. She has also written books based on the Nick Jr. shows, *Eureeka's Castle* and *Gullah Gullah Island*.

Nancy knows exactly how Didi and Stu feel in their crowded little home because she lives in an apartment in Manhattan. She shares her home with her husband Danny, two kids—Amanda and Ian—a canary named Tweety, and a very squeaky guinea pig called Tutankhamen.